Lizzie Dripping

Lizzie Dripping has always got her head in the clouds and wanders around thinking of ways she can make her life more exciting. She comes up with so many tales that nobody in the village believes her when she says she's met a witch in the churchyard— but this time she's really telling the truth.

But when she leaves the witch in charge of her baby brother things don't turn out quite as planned and Lizzie feels that the only way to make amends could be to run away from home . . .

Lizzie Dripping has had her own major television series and is a funny and entertaining character that everyone will love to read about.

Helen Cresswell was born in Nottingham and graduated in English Honours from King's College, London. *The Piemakers* was her first children's book and was nominated for the Carnegie Medal. She is also noted for the wickedly humorous *Bagthorpe Saga* and is a leading writer of children's television drama, twice BAFTA nominated. As well as the hugely successful television series of *Lizzie Dripping*, Helen has also adapted other work for television such as *The Phoenix and the Carpet* by E. Nesbit and *The Demon Headmaster* by Gillian Cross. She lives and works in a small Nottinghamshire village.

Lizzie Dripping

Other Oxford Children's Modern Classics

Lizzie Dripping

Helen Cresswell

Illustrated by Tony Ross

OXFORD
UNIVERSITY PRESS

OXFORD
UNIVERSITY PRESS

Great Clarendon Street, Oxford OX2 6DP

Oxford University Press is a department of the University of Oxford.
It furthers the University's objective of excellence in research, scholarship,
and education by publishing worldwide in

Oxford New York

Auckland Bangkok Buenos Aires
Cape Town Chennai Dar es Salaam Delhi Hong Kong Istanbul
Karachi Kolkata Kuala Lumpur Madrid Melbourne Mexico City Mumbai
Nairobi São Paulo Shanghai Taipei Tokyo Toronto

Oxford is a registered trade mark of Oxford University Press
in the UK and in certain other countries

British Library Cataloguing in Publication Data available

ISBN 0 19 271941 6

1 3 5 7 9 10 8 6 4 2

Typeset by AFS Image Setters Ltd, Glasgow

Printed in Great Britain by
Mackays of Chatham plc, Chatham, Kent

For Mary and Dennis, Catherine and Mark

Contents

Lizzie Dripping and the Orphans

Once upon a time—and I mean last week, or last year—there was a girl called Lizzie Dripping. There is a girl called Lizzie Dripping in most villages round these parts. It isn't meant unkindly, it's really quite affectionate. It fits the kind of girl who is dreamy and daring at the same time, and who turns things upside down and inside out wherever she goes and whatever she does.

This is how *our* Lizzie Dripping was. She walked about with her head in the clouds and was

1

always trying to make life more exciting, more full of shivers and panics and laughter than it is if you leave it to itself. It often looked as if she was telling what most people would call fibs. She wasn't, of course. She was just making things up as she went along—and that is quite a different thing.

Lizzie's real name was Penelope Arbuckle, but no one ever called her that. There was her father, Albert Arbuckle, whose real trade was that of a blacksmith but who worked as a plumber most of the time because there were more burst pipes to be mended than horses to be shod these days. There was her mother, Patty, who had her feet as firmly planted on the ground as Lizzie had her head stuck in the air, so that it was a wonder that the two of them ever met. And then there was the baby, Toby, who at the time we are talking about was little more than a gurgle—and a yell.

'My little fat lamb', Patty called him—and fat he certainly was.

One autumn evening the Arbuckles were sitting round the living-room fire after supper. Patty was patching a pair of trousers, and Lizzie was reading a comic on the sofa next to Albert, who was behind his newspaper. There came a knock on the door.

'Come in!' cried Patty, without getting up. The back door opened straight into the little room. First a face peered round, then the rest of the visitor followed.

'Blodwen!' cried Patty. 'You come right in and shut the door. Move off, Lizzie, and make room for your Aunt Blod.'

Blodwen was not Lizzie's aunt at all, not strictly speaking. She was just one of Patty's oldest friends, and had wormed her way into the family, so Lizzie thought, by false pretences.

'Nippy out, it is,' she announced, plumping herself on the end of the sofa nearest the fire. 'Frost next thing, I shouldn't wonder. Burst pipes, Albert!'—giving him a nudge.

'Early yet for that, Blodwen,' he replied. 'Too much wind about. Don't reckon on much in the way of burst pipes while Christmas.'

'Leeks going all right, are they?' she enquired.

'Insofar as I can tell, Blodwen, while I dig 'em up.'

'Grows a lovely leek, Patty, don't he? Best leek grower in Little Hemlock, that's what I always tell people. Cup of tea going, is there?' She knew the family well enough to ask a question like this when it was quite obvious that there was *not* a cup of tea going.

'Soon can be, Blod,' replied Patty, getting up.

She put the kettle to boil on the hob, then sat down again.

'Drat!' she cried. 'Whatever's that?'

'That' was Toby yelling.

'Drat that child!' she cried. 'It's as if he *knowed* every time I put the kettle on. I've only to sit down and rest my legs over a cup of tea, and he sets up as if bottom had dropped out of his cot. Nip up, Lizzie, there's a good girl, and turn him over.'

I'll turn him over, Lizzie thought. Blodwen ain't come here for a cup o' tea, she's come to *tell* something, and I want to hear it told.

She raced up the narrow stairs and had no sooner reached the top than Toby's yelling stopped as abruptly as it had started.

Well if *that* ain't just like him, and all, she thought. Drat you, Toby Arbuckle, for a blessed nuisance.

Back in the living-room she was just in time to hear Blodwen say, ' . . . for the orphans, bless their little hearts.'

'What orphans?' demanded Lizzie.

'All orphans,' Blodwen said. 'All the poor little children without so much as either a mother or father as *you're* lucky to have, Lizzie Dripping.'

'Your aunt was telling us about the Bring and Buy there's to be,' explained Patty, busying

4

herself with cups and saucers. 'You'll have a slice of seed cake, won't you, Blodwen? Bring and Buy in Chapel Hall in aid of the orphans, she says.'

'Bring and Buy,' Blodwen nodded. 'November seventh, Chapel Hall at six-thirty. Usual stalls, you know, plenty of cakes and knitting. Only thing is, it's *toys* we want most of, see. Toys.'

'Hurray!' cried Lizzie. 'I'm saving up, then!'

'Toys to *give*, it is, Lizzie,' said Blodwen severely. 'Surprised at you, I am. All them toys you've got, and a mam and dad the best in the world. That's what we thought, Patty, see. All the children to give their toys to show thankful how lucky they are. Saddest thing in the world it is, to be an orphan.'

'Bless their hearts,' Patty added.

'How do you know?' asked Lizzie. 'You've never been one.'

'You shush up!' said Patty sharply. 'Speaking to your aunt like that. And you go up to your room this very minute. You just sit up there and *think* of how it feels to have no mother and father and all on your own in the world. *You'd* not get far on your own, my girl!'

Lizzie got up sulkily and went to the door.

'And you have a good sort through your things!' called Patty after her. 'Or I'll do it for you! All that stuff you've got, and grudging them to an orphan! I'm ashamed of you!'

Lizzie stamped up the stairs, though the nearer she got to the top the softer she stamped. She was mad and sorry now, but if Toby woke, she'd be madder and sorrier.

In her room there was a nearly finished jigsaw on her chest of drawers, and she stood and slotted a few pieces in while she calmed down.

Orphans don't have people *nagging* at 'em morning to night, she thought. Nag nag nag. And I *haven't* got a lot of stuff, either. Becky Farmer's got *twice* what I've got. *And* Dawn Walker. And as for that Michael Davey! Brand-new bike he had for his birthday, *and* a cricket bat, *and* roller skates. Spoilt to death, he is. *I'm* not spoilt.

She slotted in the last piece of sky.

Wish I was.

The jigsaw was finished except for the three missing pieces. It was cold up there in her room.

Better just pretend to sort through, she thought. Then I can go down. Just my luck to miss seed cake!

She knelt on the cold linoleum and dragged a big box from under the bed, noisily, to make sure they heard downstairs. She picked out a glove puppet of a bear and waggled it on her hand.

'Not parting with *that*.' She put a frog puppet on the other hand and wagged it at the bear. '*Nor* that.'

With a deep sigh she took them off.

'Now what . . . ? Paints . . . ? No. Farmyard . . . ? No. Half missing, any road. What's this? Clean forgot I had it.'

And so on, right to the bottom of the box. It was an interesting half-hour, because Lizzie really had forgotten what she had—she even found the missing pieces to the jigsaw. Then she stowed everything back again into the box and pushed it under the bed.

'I can't spare 'em,' she muttered to herself. 'I might *need* them one day. Better get down there, or seed cake'll've all gone.'

Had she known it—it already had. And it was lucky that Lizzie had not heard the conversation that was taking place downstairs while she was up above.

'She's a long time up there, our Lizzie,' said Patty. 'Sounds like she is having a sort through—and none too soon, either. The stuff she's got up there you wouldn't believe. Enough to keep a dozen orphans happy.'

'You come down too hard on 'er you do, Patty,' said Albert, coming out again from behind his paper. 'She's a good lass, at bottom, and'd give her last penny, if need be.'

'Got to train 'em though, haven't you?' said Blodwen (who having no children of her own

was not biased on the subject). 'Got to make 'em *realize*?'

'A good heart don't come by training, Blodwen,' said Albert. 'And that's what our Lizzie's got—a good heart. Worth a deal of training, is that.'

'I'm not denying, Albert, I'm not *denying*!' Her mouth was full of seed cake. 'Lovely cake this, Patty. Melts in your mouth that you hardly know you've had it.'

'Have another lump, duck.' Patty offered the plate.

'Some left for Lizzie, is there?' said Albert, but too late. And Lizzie came in just in time to see the last piece being whisked off the plate by Blodwen's sharp Welsh fingers.

'Tempting me, is it, Patty Arbuckle!' she cried archly. 'And me on a diet, and all!'

Last piece, thought Lizzie. Trust her. First diet *I've* ever heard of wi' half a seed cake in it.

'Oh! Back, are you?' Blodwen's voice was sharp even through the cake.

'Is there any more cake, Mum?' asked Lizzie. 'I'm hungry.'

'Hungry now, is it?' cried Blodwen. 'And what about the poor little orphans, I should like to know? Had a good think about them, I hope, and the terrible lives they lead?'

'Thinking don't stop me getting hungry,' said Lizzie. 'Is there any, Mum?'

'You sit and wait,' Patty told her. 'Had a good clear-out, did you? Where's the stuff for the Bring and Buy?'

'I'm still deciding,' said Lizzie. 'I ain't got to decide tonight, have I?'

Blodwen was shaking her head. 'Pity is she never had a brother or sister, Patty. Trouble with an only child, that is. Selfish. Not used to sharing, see.'

'I have then!' cried Lizzie. 'I've got Toby!'

'Not a *proper* brother, though, is he? Only a *baby*.'

9

'Might be now, Blodwen,' said Albert, 'but he'll grow, if you give 'im time. And I shouldn't say our Lizzie's been spoilt. She's a good lass she is.'

'I'm not denying, Albert, I'm not *denying*! All I say is that for an only child it's difficult, see. Very difficult.' She paused, and popped the last bite of seed cake delicately into her mouth. 'One of seven, I was!'

And I bet the other six never saw much seed cake! Lizzie had to think the thought, because she dared not say it. After that nobody said anything more about the toys, almost as if they found Lizzie's behaviour so shocking that it was hardly even to be spoken about. She was glad when it was bedtime.

It seemed to Lizzie as she hurriedly undressed and slipped into bed, that it had been a dreadful evening, and that no orphan on earth could possibly have had a worse one.

But the strange thing was that once Lizzie was lying in bed, and beginning to feel pleasantly warm and drowsy, she began to think, for the first time, about the orphans. Lizzie always did a great deal of her dreaming and thinking in bed, just before she fell asleep, and tonight, try as she might to push the thought away, she simply could not help thinking about what it would really be like to be an orphan.

All on your own in the world, she thought,

remembering Patty's words. The wind was moaning in the near-leafless boughs of the giant beeches away down below, and she pulled the bedclothes higher over her ears.

The picture of an orphan that began to form in her mind was of a little barefoot girl, dressed only in rags, wandering lost out there in the wind and cold. An owl hooted down below and Lizzie gave a little shiver. A moment later there came an answering call. And to Lizzie, who had lain and listened to the owls hooting a hundred times before, their calls tonight seemed unbearably sad and lonely.

'Who . . . whooooooo?'

As if they were asking the same question as the little ragged girl who ran here and there outside in the darkness, knocking vainly on doors, looking for her lost father and mother. And as she watched the girl, gradually she began to see not only the streaming rags and the bare legs and feet, but the *face*.

Slowly it changed from a pale blur into a face, and it was a face that she recognized, and all at once Lizzie realized that it was *herself*, her very own face. And she could see tears running down, and at the same time felt warm trickles run from her own eyes and on to the pillow where they straightaway grew cold.

'Poor little orphan,' she cried softly. '*Poor* little thing,' and as she cried she was crying for herself, running barefoot out there in the dark and seeing the curtains of the windows all drawn tight and no one to see or take pity on her.

Again the owl hooted.

Lizzie pushed back the covers and snapped on the light, blinking and brushing her eyes on the back of her hand.

'I'll give you some toys!' she cried to herself. 'Wait—*I'll* give you some!'

She ran over the cold lino to the cupboard where she kept her best toys, the ones she really loved, the ones she had never even looked at when she had come up earlier that night. Swiftly she sorted among them, picking things out—one here, one there. She took out the monkey with the tattered fur that Albert had won for her at the Goose Fair five years ago. She picked out the one-eared rabbit called Loppy, the tiny Japanese doll, and the beautiful tin teapot with painted sunflowers. She put them in a pile on top of the cupboard, turned off the light and got back into bed.

Before long the picture of the orphan began to float up again, but this time, as the picture began to grow clearer, she could see that the girl was standing with the toys held tightly in her arms, and was smiling over them straight into Lizzie's eyes. Lizzie smiled back, and fell asleep.

In the morning when she awoke, the first thing she saw was the pile of toys. Then she remembered the ragged orphan who had run barefoot in the night through her dreams. Now, in the light of day, the orphan seemed very unreal and far away, and she felt a pang as she remembered how she had promised her toys— given them, as good as.

'Have to stick to it now, Lizzie,' she said to herself. 'Can't back down now.'

When she got up she sadly put the toys together into a brown paper carrier and put it back into the cupboard. She tried not to think about it during the days that followed, and most of the time, succeeded.

The day came for the Bring and Buy. Patty was up early as she always was on such occasions. She was baking nearly all day, because her drop scones and bakewell tarts were famous, and always sold out first, even at two pence each. She was still baking in the afternoon when Lizzie came in from a skipping session in the yard.

'Mmm! Smells nice, Mum!'

'Now you needn't start that, Lizzie,' said Patty.

'I know what you're after, right enough. For the orphans, these cakes, not great girls like you that's eat, eat, eating from morning till night, and never satisfied, seemingly.'

'I know, Mum. What I meant was—lucky orphans. You're best cook in Little Hemlock, Mum—even Becky Farmer says that.'

'Hmmm.' Patty was pleased, despite herself. 'Well, that's as maybe. I know I've always to be up at crack of dawn baking if ever there's a Bring and Buy in this here village. You got them toys ready, Lizzie, for when your Aunt Blodwen comes?'

'Here, Mum.' Lizzie showed her the bag standing by her chair. She could see Midge's head sticking out from the top.

'There's a good girl,' said Patty. 'I knew you would, when you'd time to think about it. And you've that much stuff—*I* never had that much stuff when I was your age.'

'Mum . . . Why do I have to call her *Auntie* Blodwen? She i'n't my real aunt at all, is she?'

'That's a nice thing to come up with, for goodness' sake!' cried Patty. 'Called her Auntie ever since you was old enough to talk, and now—'

A knock came at the door. It was the one Lizzie had been dreading all day.

'Come in!' cried Patty.

As if we don't know who *that* is, thought Lizzie.

'Mmmm!' cried Blodwen. 'Lovely smell! Halfway up the street I smelt it! Try one, can I?' and had whisked up a bakewell and bitten into it before Lizzie had so much as opened her mouth to say: 'For the orphans, them! Two pence each to you!' under her breath.

Blodwen nodded at Lizzie, who scowled back.

Just look at her! Lizzie thought. Easy to get *other* people giving things for orphans. An orphan could've done with that tart—'n so could I, for that matter!

'Got your toys sorted, have you?' asked Blodwen thickly, through a mouthful of crumbs.

Without answering, Lizzie picked up the bag of toys and passed them over.

'There's a good girl!' cried Blodwen. 'Isn't she, Patty? See what you've given, shall we?'

'Let them alone! Let my things alone, old busybody! It's the orphans they're for, and none of your business!' But she said the words silently.

She watched Blodwen's fingers prying into the bag. The monkey came out first, bald patches, dangling tail and all.

'Oh, Midge!' cried Lizzie silently. 'Goodbye, Midge!'

15

'Ooooh!' Blodwen's exclamation sounded surprised and disappointed at once.

'Whatever . . . ? Oooooh . . . ! No ear to it, this rabbit hasn't. Bit scratched, isn't it?' This, picking up the beautiful sunflower teapot. 'It's not your *rubbish* you're giving, I hope, after all that was said?'

'What?' Patty looked up. 'Midge? Giving him, are you? Never thought to see the day we'd see back of *him*. *And* that mangy old rabbit. Good riddance.'

She sounded pleased. At that moment, Lizzie did not know which one of them she hated most.

'Not a *jumble* sale, this,' said Blodwen, offended now. '*Nice* toys it was we were after—money we're trying to raise, for all them little orphans, bless their hearts! Hardly two pence each these'll fetch, I should doubt. However!'

She picked up the bag and went to the door, 'See you later, then!' and was gone.

Lizzie stared after her, aghast. 'Mum!' she cried. 'They're going to sell them! She said they're going to *sell them*!'

Patty looked up, startled.

'Whatever else, Lizzie Dripping? Not that there'll be more than ten pence for that lot. Could've given *one* decent thing, Lizzie.'

Lizzie hardly heard. 'But they're for the

orphans! I gave 'em for the orphans! I wanted 'em to have *my* toys!'

'*Money's* for orphans,' said Patty. 'Toys are to be sold for money to give to the orphans. Same thing, isn't it? I don't know what you're going on about, Lizzie, really I don't. Now come along, there's a good girl, and get these counted into half-dozens. You'll get bags from the pantry.'

Dazed, Lizzie did as she was told. And all the time she was thinking, Gone! Gone for ever now, Midge and Loppy and my beautiful teapot! And to *sell* them. Heaven knows who'll get 'em!

It was almost too much to bear. And worst of all was the picture that Lizzie had of the orphan, running through the darkness with her arms outstretched for the promised toys that would never be hers now. Never . . .

Patty told Albert all about it when he came home.

'Proper upset she was,' she said. 'Crying, you could see that. And I must say I never thought to see the day when she'd part wi' that monkey—*or* that rabbit.'

'Fond on 'em,' agreed Albert, spearing a sausage and balancing baked beans over it. 'Won that monkey for 'er meself at the Goose Fair, as I remember, on a coconut shy. See her face now I can, when I give it her. Lit up like a Christmas tree it did.'

'Oh, go on, Albert Arbuckle,' said Patty. 'Great soft thing. Getting a big girl now, Lizzie is, and time she parted with all that baby stuff.'

'Dunno about *baby* stuff,' said Albert. 'Fond of 'em, that's the point. Like me and my leeks.'

'I can see you sending *them* to a Bring and Buy,' Patty told him tartly. 'You wouldn't send 'em to save your own grandmother, let alone orphans.'

'Now that ain't true, Patty,' said Albert. 'I'm reet fond o' my leeks, and I don't deny it. But it don't say as I wouldn't part wi' 'em, if needs be necessary. And my grandmother, Patty, is dead, as you'll remember, and not to be spoken light of.'

'Now, 'twas only a manner o' speaking, Albert, you know that.'

'All I say is,' said Albert, 'that lass's given things she were reet fond of, and credit to her. Might have looked nowt much to us, like, but they meant a lot to our Lizzie, and no mistake about it. Where is she, then? Gone over to t' Chapel Hall, has she?'

'Aye. Went to get there when it opened. Come back wi' a load of rubbish as usual, I don't doubt.'

'Now there you go again, Patty, love,' said

Albert. 'Might *seem* rubbish, to you and me, but it's summat she wants. I mind when I was a lad, there was this here teddy bear—Piggle, I used to call 'im, or Poggle—aye, that's it—Poggle!'

'You!' cried Patty, laughing. 'A teddy bear? *Poggle?*'

'Aye,' replied Albert, with dignity, 'and no reason why not, for aught I can see. And this here teddy, I'd as soon be parted from 'im as from me own mother. I kept that creature till his stuffing dropped out, and his hair dropped and he'd only one eye—aye, I mind that—give him a kind of rascal look, did that. Aye . . . '

'Great soft thing you are, Albert Arbuckle,' said Patty. 'You wi' your teddies. I half begin to see where our Lizzie gets it from. Now if I leave the pudding in the oven, Albert love, help yourself, will you? It's gone half past six now, and I shall miss all t'bargains.'

She took off the pinafore that was protecting her new brown crimplene dress and patted her hair in front of the half-silvered mirror over the mantelshelf.

Then the door flew open. There stood Lizzie Dripping, her thin face pink and shining, beaming, over an armful of toys. A bald monkey, a one-eared rabbit, a Japanese doll, and a tin teapot with sunflowers on it.

'Look! Mum! Dad! I bought 'em all back! I bought 'em back, all of 'em! And only two pence each, just like Aunt Blodwen said! They're all mine again—and orphans have't money and all!'

Albert and Patty, struck dumb, stared at her. And if *they* had seen the orphan of Lizzie's dreams, they would have recognized her now, standing here in front of them, come in from out the cold . . .

That night, Lizzie took the toys and put them back in the bag where she had been saving them. She climbed into bed, put out the light, and shut her eyes. And almost at once she began to see the orphan girl, running again in her tattered rags.

'I've still got 'em,' whispered Lizzie. 'And I'll save 'em for you! Don't worry—I'll save 'em!'

And the orphan girl smiled, and Lizzie smiled back, and fell asleep.

Lizzie Dripping and the
Witch

That day, Lizzie did not feel like walking back with the others after school. Becky Farmer called to her, but Lizzie pretended not to hear.

Wants to play hospitals, she thought. Sick of that game, I am. Only just got those spots washed off me she did with her felt tips *last* time.

So she hung round, waiting to be the last to go, and thinking that perhaps she could walk along with Miss Platt.

'What is it, Lizzie?' asked Miss Platt, appearing behind her. 'Have you forgotten something?'

'I was wondering if I could wait and walk along with you. I could show you that marrow I was telling you about—in Mr Briggs's garden. Honest, Miss Platt, it's the biggest I ever saw. I keep wondering if it's going to end up biggest there's ever been in the *world*. Going to put it in church for Harvest Festival, he says, but rate it's going he won't get it in through't *door*!'

Miss Platt laughed, but not in the way some people might have laughed. A *proper* laugh, she had.

'Why, thank you,' she said. 'I'd love to see it, Lizzie, and you shall show it to me. But I have your books to mark before I go home. And I think Becky's waiting for you. I should go and play with her, outside, while the weather holds.'

'Don't feel like it,' said Lizzie. 'Don't always feel like playing, you know.'

'I know,' said Miss Platt. 'It's nice to be alone sometimes.'

'Oh, I'm not *alone*!' cried Lizzie. 'Least, I—oh, I dunno! Bye, Miss Platt!'

Becky Farmer beckoned to her as she went out through the school gate, but Lizzie shook her head and went in the other direction.

Go home and get an apple or summat, she

thought, and that book on giants, then I'll go to the Pingle, and sit and read under't beeches.

Patty was in the kitchen ironing.

'You, is it, Lizzie?' she said. 'Nice day, was it?'

She said the same thing every day, and Lizzie often had the feeling that she never listened to the answer.

'Smashing,' she said. 'We did collage things, with leaves and nuts and that. Look!'

She held it up. It was all brown and gold and tattered—just *like* autumn, which was what it was supposed to be.

'Hmmm. Very nice. But don't leave it down here, Lizzie. It'll get sat on.'

Lizzie held it up again. 'Look, Dad!'

'That's real good, our Lizzie,' said Albert, putting down his newspaper. 'You've made a real pretty picture of it. Hang it on the wall, shall you?'

'Not in here, Albert, if you please,' said Patty. 'Clutter enough, without leaves on walls.'

'Put it in your room, love, that's best,' said Albert. 'Look nice, that will.'

'Till leaves start dropping off,' said Patty tartly. The steam flew up out of the iron in clouds. 'Till't leaves start dropping off and all over't floor for me to sweep up. Now nip up to't shop, Lizzie, will you, and fetch some butter.'

Bang go my giants, thought Lizzie. Might've known.

'Here's money.' Patty handed it over. 'Look sharp now, Lizzie, we shall be wanting it teatime.'

So Lizzie went up to the shop and bought the butter, and as she walked slowly back home down Kirk Street, she all of a sudden had the feeling that she would like a walk around the graveyard. And being Lizzie, it was no sooner thought than done. She scrambled up the bank by the memorial cross and next minute was through the little swing gate into the graveyard itself. She stopped dead.

You really could not believe your eyes. You could *not*, absolutely not, walk up your own street on a hot September afternoon, turn into the graveyard for a quiet half-hour, and see a witch sitting there.

Lizzie saw the witch before the witch saw her. What the witch was doing, was sitting with her back propped against a tombstone—the one in memory of *Hannah Post of this parish and Albert Cyril beloved husband of the above 1802 to 1879 Peace Perfect Peace.* Lizzie was not sure which shocked her most—seeing a witch at all, or seeing a witch propped against a tombstone.

Nobody should sit, lean, or stand upon a

tombstone. It showed disrespect for the dead. Lizzie herself sometimes did all three of these things, but never *carelessly*, as if it didn't matter. When *she* sat on a tombstone, it was with a thudding heart and a pounding sense of wickedness that would have made it quite impossible for her to do a single row of knitting or read so much as a page of a book.

And the witch was doing both. She sat in a black, untidy heap with a book propped open against a little marble flower pot that Lizzie was *sure* had been moved from the nearby grave of *Betsy Mabel Glossop aged 79 years Life's Work Well Done.*

Her hands, which were the only part of her that showed, kept making awkward jerking stabs with a pair of long wooden pins from which hung a length of lacy, soot-black knitting. Either it was lacy, or full of holes. Holes, probably, Lizzie decided. The witch did not look at all a good knitter.

The longer she stood there, the more Lizzie wondered whether she was actually seeing what she seemed to be seeing. She closed her eyes for a moment, then opened them again. She saw the crooked stones, green with moss, she saw the tall cow parsley with its seeding heads, she saw the roof of Pond Farm in the dip below. And she saw a black bundle topped with a pointed hat propped against the tombstone of the Perfectly Peaceful Posts. She saw a witch.

Lizzie turned and went softly back along the little path by the church, through the gate and back into Kirk Street, hot and shadowless and smelling of the blue smoke from the burning stubble. No one was about except Jake Staples, who was not really worth talking to. He was playing marbles with himself outside his house. Lizzie stood over him for a minute, watching him cheat.

'Hello,' she said. 'Who's winning?'

'Me,' said Jake.

It struck Lizzie that perhaps Jake was the one person in Little Hemlock who *would* believe there was a witch in the churchyard. After all, he had believed her the time she had told him his house was on fire. He had left off knocking conkers down from Mrs Adams's chestnut and gone running down the village like ten furies. (Leaving Lizzie, who often had a *reason* for fibbing, to pick up his pile of conkers and stow them in her own bag.)

'There's a witch in the graveyard,' she told him now.

'And pigs can fly,' replied Jake, killing two marbles in one go. 'Cats've got five legs. Monkeys are bl—' (He was going to say 'blue'.)

'I tell you there is,' she said.

'You go away, Lizzie Dripping,' said Jake. 'I'm busy.'

'And don't you dare call me that!' she cried.

'Everyone else does. Lizzie Dripping! My ma says you're a fibber and I'm not to talk to you.'

'You say that once more,' said Lizzie, 'and I'll kick your marbles flying. I'll kick them to the four corners of the earth!'

She liked saying that, because she knew for a fact that the earth was round and didn't *have* any corners. Jake began to pick his marbles up and stuff them rapidly into his pockets.

'I'm going to tell my ma about you,' he said.

'And I'm going to tell that witch about you!' returned Lizzie.

She marched back towards the church. Once out of sight and past the gate, she tiptoed. It was one thing to see a witch, and quite another to let a witch see you.

There she still sat, in a great black hunch. Lizzie stepped off the path behind a particularly large, show-off slab in memory of one of *The Petersons of the Manor*. The soft buff plumes of seeding grass brushed her bare legs.

'I spy with my little eye!' said a voice.

Lizzie leapt and banged her knee hard against the stone.

'Owch!'

'Saw you the first time, and I see you now,' came the same cracked, chatty voice. The fingers were still stabbing with the needles, the face still hidden under that wide black brim.

Lizzie stood poised. Should she run or should she stay? She wanted, despite the knocking of her knees and the thudding of her heart, to stay. She knew for a fact that in all Little Hemlock there was no one half so interesting to talk to as this witch.

'If *I* was going to hide,' the voice went on, 'I should vanish into thin air.'

Lizzie stepped from behind the stone.

'What, knitting and all?' she asked, interested.

For answer, the witch vanished. Lizzie blinked. She could still smell clover and nettles, and the pigeons were still crooning in the yews, and at the far end of the village she could hear the chimes of the ice-cream van.

'I am definitely awake,' she said to herself, and as if to prove it, stepped sideways and stung her leg on a nettle.

'Owch!' she cried again, rubbing it. 'So that's that,' she said out loud at last. 'Seeing one of my own fibs, I expect.'

Lizzie was a very *honest* fibber.

Then the witch was there again, still knitting.

'You *are* there!' cried Lizzie.

'Knit one, slip one, knit one, pass the slip stitch over,' said the witch. 'Of course I am. And I'm fed up with knitting. Fiddling, baby clothes is. Fiddle fiddle fiddle.'

She plunged the spare needle fiercely into the black cobweb, fished for the ball of wool, and stowed them all into a pocket somewhere in her black robes.

'The thing is,' said Lizzie, choosing her words carefully. 'There are no such things as witches.'

'That's all right, then, isn't it?' said the witch. 'Come a little closer, and I'll turn you into a toad.'

Lizzie let out a little squeal and clapped her hand to her mouth.

'I'm sorry!' she cried. 'I didn't mean to be rude!'

The witch looked up then. Her face certainly looked like what a witch's face would look like if there were such things as witches.

'Try me,' she said.

'T-try you?' repeated Lizzie.

'Tell me something to do. A test.'

'You mean a *spell*?'

Lizzie felt a swift shiver under the hot sun. Could a spell happen in Little Hemlock, on her own doorstep?

'I—I don't know if I want to, actually, thank you,' she said at last.

'Rubbish!' snapped the witch. 'You're dying to, girl!'

It was true. The fibbing part of Lizzie, the part of her that wanted to believe in everything and anything under the sun, was itching. It was itching to see the impossible actually *happen*.

'Come along,' said the witch. 'I haven't got all day.'

'Just a minute,' said Lizzie. 'Let me think.'

Quick. Think. Blank. Nothing. The best fibber in Little Hemlock stuck for an idea. Lizzie Dripping, of all people!

'In a minute,' said the witch, beginning to sound dangerous, '*I* shall think of something.'

'Oh! Oh dear!' Lizzie was frantic. 'What about . . . what about . . . ?'

She was hedging for time.

'What about what?' enquired the witch relentlessly.

'What-about-turning-that-bird-into-a-toad?'

It all came out in a rush. She didn't feel herself *think* it, only heard herself *say* it. Somewhere at the back of her mind she had the idea that witches specialized in turning things into toads. And if anything round here was going to be turned into a toad, she didn't want to be it.

'What? Is that all?' The witch sounded disappointed.

'Which bird?' She scanned about her with eyes that looked oddly short-sighted for a witch. As if reading Lizzie's thoughts (and a chill ran down Lizzie's back), she dug into her robes and fished out a pair of spectacles.

'Which bird?' she repeated, looking about her over the rims.

'Th-that one!' Lizzie really did not care. She picked on an unsuspecting thrush sitting halfway up a yew that hung over the grave of Robert Miller (*Come Unto Me All Ye That Labour*).

Poor thrush! she thought fleetingly, just in time to see it turn toad.

She clapped a hand to her mouth.

'Hmmmm!' she heard the witch's mutter. 'Not much to *that*. Any more?'

She picked on a robin, worming by a granite cross.

'Oh!' Lizzie gasped again. 'Poor robin!'

There were two toads now. One by the cross and one halfway up the yew. The one in the yew looked startled, even for a toad.

'Oh! Turn them back, can't you?' she cried. 'Look at that poor thing up the tree—oooh! Look out—it's going to jump!'

It did, too. And what was even more surprising, landed safely. It certainly looked bewildered, staring out among the grasses on the grave of Robert Miller (*Come Unto Me All Ye That Labour*), but more at home than up in the tree.

'T'ain't nature, toads in trees,' remarked the witch.

For all the world, thought Lizzie, as if turning birds into toads *was* nature!

'Now what?' asked the witch impatiently.

Now she's started spelling, thought Lizzie, how on earth am I going to stop her?

Desperately she racked her brains for something interesting but *safe*. After all, the witch had turned the birds *into* toads, but there was no guarantee at all that she would—or even could—turn them back again.

P'raps I'd better find out, she thought.

'What about turning them back?' she suggested.

The witch looked disappointed.

'Back? Already? Bird to toad, toad to bird? Child's play. Waste a witch's time, would you?'

Sulkily she snapped her fingers again and muttered under her breath. Next minute the two surprised-looking toads were two surprised-looking birds. They flew off—right off and on out of sight. Lizzie watched them go—and hardly blamed them.

'Now what?' said the witch again. 'And not toads, this time.'

Lizzie's brain went blank again. Quick. Think.

'Don't believe in me, girl, do ye?' snapped the witch. '*I* know. *I* can tell.'

'Of c-course I do!'

The witch sniffed.

'*My* turn, any hows,' she said. 'Turn and turn about. *My* turn to choose a spell.'

'Oh—oh dear! All right, then!' cried Lizzie a little desperately. She crossed her fingers, on both hands.

'Now you see one!' cried the witch. 'And now you see *three*!'

'Oooooh!' Lizzie let out a shrill squeal. Facing her in a row, like ravens on a bough, were *three* witches! Lizzie blinked rapidly, in case there was something in her eye that was making her see treble. But there was no doubt about it at all. Propped against the tombstone of the Perfectly Peaceful Posts were three definite, distinct witches.

Her own witch—the one in the middle— looked pleased.

'That's more like home,' she remarked. 'And three can spell easier than one, eh, girls?'

The other two cackled merrily.

If all three of them do *that* spell, thought

35

Lizzie in a panic, then there'll be *nine* witches. And if *they* all do it, there'll be twenty-seven, and if *they* all do it, there'll be—but her arithmetic gave out. Instead of a number, all she came up with was a terrible picture of Little Hemlock churchyard thick with spelling witches—*blackened* with them.

Lizzie was desperate. Her mother had told her time and again that she should never speak to strangers. But why, oh *why*, had she not warned her never, ever, to speak to witches?

'*Now* do you believe in witches?' cried Lizzie's witch triumphantly.

'I do! I do!' Lizzie cried. 'I believed in you before, really I did! But now I believe in you *three* times as much! Honestly! Really!'

'Well, then,' said the witch, 'give us a spell to do. A proper one, this time. Come along, girl.'

Lizzie Dripping's brain turned to water again.

'Speak up, girl!' snapped the witch. 'I can't hear you!'

'I—I didn't say anything!' stammered Lizzie.

What should she say? Change church into a gingerbread palace . . . ? No. Put bags of potato crisps instead of daisies . . . ? Better . . . Make her own hair grow down to her waist and be buttercup yellow instead of brown? *That* was it! Just as she'd always dreamed—two lovely long pigtails, long as Rapunzel's—or at least, long enough to sit on. She would tie them with scarlet ribbons and parade up and down Main Street. Wouldn't they all stare . . . ?

'I've thought!' she cried. 'I've got a spell for you! Make my hair—'

But she never finished.

'Lizzie Dripping! Lizzie Dripping!'

She turned quickly. It was Jake Staples, there by the gate.

'Thought you said there was a witch!' he yelled. 'Witch my foot! Witch my elbow! Witch yourself!

Lizzie Dripping, Lizzie Dripping,
Don't look now, your fibs are slipping!
Lizzie Dripping, Lizzie Dripping,
Don't l—'

'Go away!' she screamed. 'Go away this minute! You'll spoil—'

She turned back to where the witches were, and stopped dead.

'Oooooh!' She let out her breath in a long gasp. Where the witches were—the witches weren't.

Gone. Vanished—as only witches *can* vanish. From one moment to the next, into thin air . . .

'Lizzie Dripping, Lizzie Dripping!'

Jake was still calling, but she hardly heard him.

'Oh witch,' she whispered. 'Where are you?'

She stared at the tombstone of the Perfectly Peaceful Posts as if by staring hard enough, and long enough, she could *make* her reappear. Jake had stopped calling now, and there was no sound but for the purr of pigeons and the rustle of wind in the dry grasses.

Slowly, very slowly, she advanced.

If she is still there—or if all three of them are still there, even if they are invisible, I might touch them . . . , she thought.

She paused. Gingerly she put out her hands, feeling the thin air. Nothing.

That witch'nd me could've been friends, she thought.

Then, very softly, she said out loud, 'Goodbye, witch. I *do* believe in you, you know, even now you're not here, and even though I don't know your name. And witch—' pause—'I'm coming back tomorrow. Will you be there . . . ?'

No answer.

'Goodbye, witch,' said Lizzie Dripping. 'Till tomorrow.'

And she turned and went home, because in her money box she had ten pence, and she wanted to buy some scarlet ribbons . . .

Lizzie Dripping's Black Sunday

One day Lizzie Dripping got out of bed and put the wrong foot down to the floor first. Some people might say she got out of bed the wrong side, but in Lizzie's case this was impossible. Her bed was next to the wall. If Lizzie had known quite how bad the day was going to be, if she had known that it was a day that she was going to think of forever afterwards as 'Black Sunday', she might not have got out of bed at all. But she did not know, so after lying for a few minutes watching the breeze stirring the curtains and hearing the sleepy croon of the pigeons, she did get out—putting the wrong foot to the floor first.

This would not have been so bad if Patty, her mother, had not put the wrong foot to the floor first as well. And if Toby, the baby, had been old enough to put his foot out of his cot, *that* would have been the wrong one, too. He had done nothing but yell since the moment he woke. (Toby did not cry—he yelled.)

It was Sunday, and that made matters worse.

'It's always the same,' Patty said, bundling Toby into his pram. 'Every blessed Sunday it's the same. Day of rest—it's enough to make the cat laugh! No more rest do I get than if I was a slave in chains.'

'Here, then, Patty,' said Albert. 'I'll put him out for you.'

He pushed the pram out into the yard where Toby still yelled, but at least at more of a distance.

The bells began to ring for the morning service. In a moment, Toby stopped yelling.

'Aaah!' Patty let out a long breath. 'That's better. That's more like a Sunday morning. Now where's my joint?'

It was the same every Sunday. As soon as Patty heard the bells ring, she remembered the joint. Half past ten it went in, half past twelve it came out, regular as clockwork.

'Time you was off to Sunday School, Lizzie,' she went on. 'You just give your hands a good wash and—' she broke off.

'Well, I declare! Lizzie Dripping, what are you thinking of? Bells going fit to bust their ropes and you not even changed! Look at you!'

'But, Mum, there *ain't* no Sunday School. I told you. Ma Parker's gone away, and said we was to read the story of Daniel in the lions' den and write it in our own words.'

Patty opened her mouth.

'And I've done it already,' said Lizzie. 'Did it last night, in bed.'

'Oh.' Patty closed her mouth again.

Albert came back in. He was not wearing the cap he wore for gardening, but his going-out cap, which meant that Patty was going to be even more annoyed.

'He'll go off, then.' With a jerk of his head.

'And none too soon.' Patty banged the cupboard door.

She stood for a moment then, dripping tin in hand, listening.

'Just hark at them bells. Takes me right back, every time I hear 'em. Right from when *I* was in a pram, I've heard them bells.'

41

Lizzie stared. Of course—Patty had been born and bred in Little Hemlock. As a baby she must have lain in her pram as Toby did now, and fallen asleep to the sound of these very bells on Sundays. It was always difficult for Lizzie to imagine her mother as a child at all. Of course, she knew she *must* have been, once, and in any case she had seen photographs to prove it. It was simply that Patty was so *organizing* that it was hard to imagine her ever having been organized herself.

Perhaps she was an organizing *baby*, Lizzie thought.

She moved vaguely to the open door and leaned there, hearing the bells come slow and beautiful over the gardens, and the footsteps go by in the street. She smelt the damp autumn earth and the first wafts of roasting fat and would have known it was a Sunday even with her eyes shut, and wondered, with a soft shiver, whether she would still be living in Little Hemlock when she grew up, and whether she would think back to her own childhood—to now . . .

'This is my childhood,' she said to herself, and found the thought quite new, and interesting, because she had always taken it for granted, never actually realized it as she did at this moment. And with the realization came another slow, soft

shiver, as another thought followed, 'Soon it won't be my childhood any more . . . '

She shut her eyes and tried to imagine this being true, tried to see herself as a grown-up person, and found it impossible—harder, even, than seeing Patty as a child. She opened her eyes again and the bells stopped ringing, and for a moment the world seemed unbearably empty and sad—frightening, even. The bells had gone, and soon so would her childhood too.

Toby started to yell. He had not been asleep at all—just listening to the bells.

'Drat!' she heard Patty say behind her. Then, 'Lizzie, I'm not having you hanging round all morning grizzling at me while I'm up to my ears. It won't do.'

Lizzie opened her mouth to say that she wasn't grizzling at anybody, that she had neither moved nor spoken for the last five minutes. She closed it again.

'You'd best go and give Toby a push round,' Patty went on. 'If I'm to make a Yorkshire pudding that'll stand up without crutches, there'll have to be a sight more quiet than this. And I can't be running out to him every five minutes. And you'll be well out of the way, I don't doubt, Albert Arbuckle.'

'I thought I'd just get over to Bilbury for an hour,' said Albert apologetically. 'For't whippet racing, like.'

'Aye, you would,' said Patty grimly. 'And what your poor mother'd've said if she'd known you was gambling money away on whippets, I don't know. And on a Sunday!'

'Now, Patty,' said Albert. 'Only a few pence. You know that.'

'Pence or pounds, makes no difference. Now come along, Lizzie, look sharp. You give him a good push round and it'll see him off till dinner.'

Lizzie sighed. 'All right, Mum.' She took the handle of the pram. 'Come on, you great fat nuisance.'

Toby yelled the louder, as if he knew an insult when he heard one, and was paying it back the only way he could.

Lizzie did not really mind going for a walk at all. In fact it was exactly what she would have chosen to do herself. There was such a heady smell to the morning, of hedge and nettles drying in a hot sun, such mingled smells of autumn and Sunday dinners, that she would have run, let alone walked. But there was Toby to be lulled off, and she knew from experience that the slower you pushed, the drowsier he became, rocked in his pram like a boat on a slow swell.

Almost as soon as the pram started to move, the yells stopped. And as Lizzie pushed him up Church Lane between the banks of bushing hemlock, she began to think again the thoughts she had while the bells were ringing.

Wonder what it feels like to be grown-up? What if I *was* grown-up, and married, and Toby was mine?

She looked doubtfully down at him and tried with all her might to feel what she would feel if she were actually his mother. She bent over and tucked his blanket more tightly around him, and said half-heartedly: 'There now, my little fat lamb, off to bye-byes,' in the special tone of voice Patty always used when talking to him. Toby, miraculously, turned on to his side and put his thumb into his mouth.

Lizzie, pleased, walked on sedately, still playing her grown-up part, and trying to think the kind of thoughts a grown-up might have.

What shall I give 'em for their tea? I know—bacon and beans on toast—that's Lizzie's favourite. Then oranges in jelly—she fair loves *that*—and I'll bake her favourite cakes this afternoon. That's what I'll do—make some doughnuts and chocolate eclairs, and some drop scones and . . .

'Hey, Lizzie!'

She turned and saw Becky Farmer and Jake Staples, each carrying a saucepan.

'Come on! We're off blackberrying!'

Lizzie was so lost in her grown-up part that before she had even time to think she heard herself say, 'No thanks! Taking Toby for a walk, bless his heart. Having trouble with his teeth, you know.'

'Oooh! You don't say so!' cried Becky. 'Hark at her! Proper little nursemaid! C'mon, Jake. Blackberries galore down by't Pingle.'

Lizzie tossed her head and walked on. She heard their voices in the distance, mocking.

'Lizzie Dripping, Lizzie Dripping,
  Don't look now, your fibs are slipping!'

Who cares? she thought. I can get my own blackberries when I want 'em. Now where was I . . . ? Yes—that's it—doing what's for tea. Now . . .

She was just beginning to get back into her dreaming again when she looked up and saw a figure approaching with a rapid, short-stepped gait.

'Oh no! It's not *her*!'

But it was. Aunt Blodwen on her way to the chapel, by the look of it, to do the flowers for the evening service. The villagers in Little Hemlock were divided fairly equally between church and chapel, and Aunt Blodwen was one of the chapel's leading lights (as well as leading soprano).

'Well, now, if it isn't you!' cried Aunt Blodwen, who seemed to Lizzie to take a perfect delight in saying the obvious, and always aroused in Lizzie herself a strong urge to say something back like: 'No—it ain't me—it's the Loch Ness Monster!'

'Asleep, is he?' remarked Blodwen, peering at the obviously slumbering Toby and pulling back the blanket to see him better.

Is now, thought Lizzie. Much more of that, and he won't be.

She noted with interest that an earwig was walking on Aunt Blodwen's shoulder out of the great bunch of dahlias and chrysanthemums she was clutching.

'Not many *blankets*,' observed Aunt Blodwen. 'Chilled, babies get, not wrapped up properly.'

'Hot, though, ain't it?' said Lizzie.

'*September*, though!' cried Aunt Blodwen. 'That's the point, Lizzie. *Autumn*, it is. Your mother knows you're out, I hope?'

'Yes,' said Lizzie. 'Told me to give him a push round, to get him off. And he *is* off.'

She could tell what Aunt Blodwen was thinking.

Thinks I'll lose him. Thinks I'll tip pram over, or something.

'Oh well, she knows best,' said Aunt Blodwen—as if she believed no such thing.

She went on, and Lizzie began to push again, when she heard Aunt Blodwen's voice again, not five yards behind her.

'Lizzie! Sunday—and not at Sunday School?'

'There is none,' said Lizzie. 'Ma Parker's away.'

'*Mrs* Parker, I should hope, Lizzie Dripping,' said Aunt Blodwen severely. 'Pity a *substitute* couldn't be found. *Believe* in children learning between right and wrong, I do. *And* keeping them off the street on a Sunday.'

'P'raps *you* could do it, Auntie Blodwen,'

suggested Lizzie innocently. 'I know it's church and not chapel, but not that much difference, is there?'

'Not—!' Aunt Blodwen's voice rose and the earwig fell off her shoulder. 'And *me*—Sunday School? I've quite enough of a Sunday with my *flowers*, thank you. And flowers behaves 'emselves. Nothing rude and ungrateful about *flowers*.'

And she stalked off, clutching her bouquet, to make the chapel beautiful.

Full of earwigs, I bet, thought Lizzie with satisfaction.

She began to push the pram on again, but now the savour had gone out of her game.

'Now where was I . . . ?' she wondered. 'Not much fun being grown-up, anyhow, if you're like *her*. But I won't grow up like that. I won't! Wonder if there's any blackberries by't old mill? Was last year . . . '

So she turned along Side Lane and crossed over to the Wellow Road. In the field by the Neville Arms a pair of beautiful white geese were performing the kind of grave minuet that geese *do* perform on sunlit days when they find the grass soft and warm under their webbed feet. Lizzie pushed the pram along the track and dragged it up the steps and right in through the open door of the mill.

Darker in here, she thought. Less likely to wake.

There was a smell of dust and dry grain and old wood, so strong and thick that Lizzie even fleetingly wondered whether *that* might wake the baby.

Then she was outside again, feeling all at once light and free and washing her hands for once and for all of the very idea of being grown-up. For the next half-hour she rambled in ever-increasing circles round the mill, looking for blackberries and eating them as she picked them.

I've nothing to put 'em in, she thought, and no point leaving 'em for birds to fetch.

Then she found the bucket, lying in the kind of deep, overgrown ditch where you would never be surprised to find *anything*. It was an old iron one, with a small hole in the bottom, but the handle was still there, and Lizzie picked it up and swung it.

'Wonder whose? Can't be wanting it, whoever it is.'

She bent and picked a handful of long grasses and stuffed them into the hole.

Do for blackberries, she thought. Mum'd be pleased, all right. Trouble is, I've eaten most of 'em round here already. Could go down to't Pingle, I s'pose, with t'others. Plenty there . . . always is. Trouble is—Toby. Green Lane's quickest way down to't Pingle, but I'd never get the pram down there.

She climbed the steps and took a look at the peacefully slumbering Toby.

Could leave him here, if only there was someone to keep an eye . . . But who . . . ?

She looked again inside the pram. Toby lay motionless, fat and rosy as a fruit himself. She looked about. Nobody. There was not even a sound in that special, Sunday silence. The quiet was actually noticeable—something in itself, not mere absence of noise.

'I spy!' came a high, cracked voice.

'The witch!' Lizzie cried, and looked about. 'Witch, witch, where are you?'

Round and about she whirled and there, propped against the flaking bricks of the mill itself where she had *never* been a moment before, sat the witch, knitting.

'Oh!' cried Lizzie. 'You *are* there!'

'Knit one, slip one, knit one, pass the slip stitch over,' replied the witch. 'Fiddle fiddle fiddle.'

'Are you really knitting baby things?' asked Lizzie, struck by a thought. 'For a witch baby?'

'Knit one, purl one, yes I am,' said the witch. 'Knit one, slip one, knit one, pass the slip stitch over, and I'm always losing my place in the pattern.'

51

'You must like babies, then?' suggested Lizzie hopefully.

'Babies is all right,' said the witch. 'I can do with babies when they're not yelling.'

'*Mine* isn't yelling,' said Lizzie eagerly. 'He's fast asleep, good as gold, and he *never* wakes up, not till it's dinner time. He's fast on, and'll stop like that for ages.'

'What baby?' enquired the witch.

'Here. In't mill. Look.'

The witch stowed her knitting in her pocket and got up. She followed Lizzie to the mill door and peered in.

'Hmmmm,' she said. 'That's how I like 'em.'

'Then could you—I mean—would you—d'ye think you could keep an *eye* on him?' cried Lizzie. 'Just for a bit? I've found this bucket, and I could get down to't Pingle with t'others and get it right full up for pies and jam.'

'I *could*,' said the witch. 'And if he *was* to yell, I could always spell him off again.'

'Aye—you could!' cried Lizzie. 'But he'll not yell, I promise you. And minute I've filled bucket, I'll be back straight up—and I could give *you* some on 'em,' she added—though doubtfully. She could not really see the witch with her sleeves rolled up, making pastry.

The witch was still looking hard at Toby.

'Shall you do it then?' asked Lizzie. 'Keep an eye on him?'

'You get off,' said the witch. 'I'll see to him.'

'Oh thank you!' cried Lizzie. 'Thank you, witch!'

And as she turned away she thought fleetingly: Though what Ma'd say—a witch for baby-sitter!

And then she ran, helter-skelter and clutching the bucket, down the long green lane that was the shortest cut past the beeches and down to the Pingle. She ran with a special, giddy, wide-legged run between the baked ruts made by tractors and the heavy-footed cattle that streamed daily and slowly up to Stokes's farm for milking.

And once there, she picked blackberries for a whole hour, but in another way it might have been a lifetime because there *was* no time—only the hot sun and whistle of birds and the dry, sharp scent of bramble leaves. She picked till the bucket was half full and she and Becky and Jake were stained with blackberry juice all over—and particularly round their mouths. Away over the fields they heard the church clock strike twelve.

'Better go,' Jake said. 'Roast pork and stuffing.'

'Same here,' said Becky.

'Beef, us,' Lizzie said. 'And Yorkshire pud.'

And they set off at a run back towards the village, hot and hungry.

'Here!' cried Lizzie, entering the kitchen. 'Blackberries, Mum! Make a pie, will you, to go with ice-cream?'

'Very nice,' said Patty, pleased. 'Good sound 'uns, by't look on it. Though you've made a proper sight of yourself, Lizzie, and ate as many as you've picked, by't look on you.'

'It'll wash off,' said Lizzie. 'What time's dinner?'

'Soon enough. Lay table, will you, Lizzie, while I thicken gravy.'

Albert came in. He came in in a special way he had, almost making himself flat, like a shadow—sliding in.

'You're back, are you?' said Patty.

'Hello, Dad,' said Lizzie. 'Seen my blackberries? Bucketful I got, and Mum's going to make a pie to have with ice-cream.'

'Very nice,' said Albert. He cleared his throat. 'Am I to fetch Toby out, Mother, and feed? He'll be wanting his dinner first, else we'll get no peace to eat us own.'

'Go on, then,' replied Patty, as if Albert did not ask this question every Sunday of his life. 'Still asleep, is he, Lizzie?'

But Lizzie was standing aghast, the fork she was holding poised in mid-air. Toby! She had forgotten him! Left him slumbering in the darkened mill where rats could get him—rats, cats, bats—*anything*!

'Lizzie?' repeated Patty sharply.

'Oooooh!' quavered Lizzie. 'Ooooh!'

This was the worst moment of her life, she knew it. They were both looking at her now, Albert enquiringly, Patty with sudden suspicion.

'If you've gone upsetting that baby—' began Patty.

'I—I ain't!' cried Lizzie. 'Honest, Mum, I didn't. He was fast on, happy as Larry, but—oooh—I've forgot him! He's still up there!'

'Up *where*?' Patty fairly shrieked. '*Where's* he up, girl?'

'Up—up in't mill,' cried Lizzie. 'I was playing being grown-up and then I got sick of it and went with t'others to pick blackberries and I'd put him in't mill and he was asleep and—oooh—I forgot him, Mum! I'll go and get him! Quick—!'

'You get after her, Albert!' she heard Patty shriek, and as she ran Albert drew level and puffed along beside her.

'Steady—lass,' he gasped. '*I* ain't no whippet. 'E ain't going to run away, you know!'

You don't know! thought Lizzie. You don't know about the witch!

And she was all the while imagining what other terrors might have befallen little fat Toby while he lay slumbering in the shadowy mill. Bats, rats, cats—kidnappers!

'Oooooh!' she actually let out a squeal at the thought, and forced her legs to run the faster, leaving Albert behind and all the dogs in Little Hemlock barking after her, or so it seemed.

She raced at last into the mill yard and stopped dead. The pram had gone, she could see at a glance.

'Oh no!' she breathed. She shut her eyes. 'Let-him-be-there-please-let-him-be-there!' She opened them again. Gone. 'Oh Dad, Dad!'

Albert halted beside her.

'It's gone! 'Tain't where I left it! Dad, Dad, he's been kidnapped! Oh Toby! Poor little Toby!'

Albert was striding towards the mill and Lizzie followed mechanically. He stood looking about him, peering this way and that into the shadows. He even looked upwards, towards the loft, as if Toby might have been snatched up by some giant spider and was hanging up there, pram and all, in a cobweb big as a hammock.

'*Where* was it you said you put 'im?'

'Here, Dad, *here*! He's gone, I tell you, gone!'

'Eeeh, he can't have done that, lass,' said Albert stolidly. Albert, unlike Lizzie, did not believe easily in disasters. (But then, neither did he hold conversations with witches.) They both stood there, looking about them, as if by merely looking hard enough they could make the pram and Toby miraculously reappear, be *there* again, and the world the right way up.

'Vanished!' said Albert, blankly.

The word struck a chord in Lizzie's numbed mind.

'Vanished! The witch!'

She saw again in her mind's eye the graveyard, and the witch coming out of thin air and there one minute and gone the next.

'Oh no!' she cried inwardly. 'No!'

She pictured the witch standing in this very place, and Toby all of a sudden started to yell. Or perhaps the witch drumming her fingers, bored and at a loose end without her knitting, and suddenly wanting to do a spell. She saw the witch mutter and snap her fingers and whoosh!—the pram gone and Toby with it.

'O witch, witch,' she whispered. 'Give 'im back! Please!'

'What's that?' said Albert. 'What d'ye say?'

'Nowt! I didn't say owt, Dad!'

And she moved a little further away and whispered again, urgently. 'I shan't tell, witch, honest. But give 'im back! Please!'

She strained her eyes into the shadowy depths of the mill for an even darker patch that might be a witch. Nothing.

Then, in the quiet, very faintly, came the sound of a baby, yelling.

'Dad! Listen!'

They stood intently and listened. It was there, quite distinctly, and it was Toby—unmistakably and positively little fat Toby, who never cried, but yelled.

Lizzie ran out of the mill and across the mill yard and on to the road—and saw Toby's pram not twenty yards away. And pushing it—of all people—Aunt Blodwen. For the first time in her whole life, Lizzie was glad to see her.

'Dad!' she screamed. 'Come on here! I've found him!'

And she ran forward and leaned over the pram and saw Toby's mouth stretched hugely and the tears running down his puffed-out cheeks, and heard hardly a word of what Aunt Blodwen was saying.

'Found him, would you believe? Found in the mill, I ask you, all by hisself in that mucky old mill, and sobbing fit to break his heart, bless him. Never in all my life, Lizzie Dripping, never in all my born days!'

'Morning, Blodwen.' It was Albert. 'Nice morning.'

'Nice morning, is it?' cried Aunt Blodwen. 'Nice now, is it, Albert Arbuckle, and your tiny, innocent little baby left abandoned for his own good, I suppose? And lucky for him I found him, too, or who knows what might have happened? Anything might've happened, the dreadful things you read in the papers!'

'Now, Blodwen,' said Albert. 'No need to carry on. There's no harm done, and less said the better. We'll be taking him along now, to get his dinner. And thank 'ee kindly.'

Firmly he took the pram and began to push it steadily towards home, Lizzie beside him.

'Well I never!' she heard Aunt Blodwen's voice floating after them. 'Never in all my life! Cool as cucumbers, the pair of them! Never in all my born days!'

And Lizzie and Albert looked sideways at each other and smiled, and Toby began to gurgle, and they kept on towards home.

Lizzie Dripping Runs Away

I t all started with Lizzie Dripping losing the baby. The fuss they had made about it, you would have thought he had been lost *forever* instead of hardly even an hour. And considering that when they found him Toby had only just begun to feel hungry, and considering that he always *was* hungry, anyway, Lizzie couldn't for the life of her see that any real harm had been done.

But during the days that followed nobody let her forget about it for a single minute. Everybody in Little Hemlock knew about it—

Aunt Blodwen had seen to that. Lizzie had been without bubble-gum for five days now, rather than go up to the village shop again and risk having people make rude remarks about it.

But it was worst at home. Patty kept bringing it into everything. That very morning, Lizzie could not find her box of chalks.

'Seen my box of chalks, Mum?' she asked Patty, who was rolling out pastry as if she were rolling her worst enemy flat. 'I want to play hopscotch.'

'Don't you go chalking on our yard,' said Patty, without looking up. 'You want to play hopscotch, you play it on the road where it belongs. Chalk on the pavement, out of my way.'

'Can't chalk anywhere,' Lizzie said. 'That's the whole point. I keep telling you. I can't find my chalks.'

'*That* don't surprise me,' retorted Patty. 'If you can go losing your own brother, you can lose anything. Wonder to me is you've got your own head left on your shoulders.'

Here we go again, thought Lizzie. On about that dratted baby again. Might have *known* she'd drag that into it.

'Nice thing if I can't rely on a great girl like you, Lizzie, to keep an eye on your brother for half an hour,' Patty went on.

Lizzie, wisely, said nothing. She simply stared glumly at her mother, waiting for the rest of it.

'Can't think where you *get* it from,' said Patty, sure enough. 'Head in the clouds, dreaming along from morning till night. Not *my* side of the family, that *is* certain.'

Nag nag nag, thought Lizzie wearily. She don't really love me at all, you can see that. Toby's all *she* cares about. Wouldn't care two pins if it'd been me that was lost.

'Pity you can't find something useful to do, instead of sitting about gawping,' said Patty, who was cutting the pastry now, making *mincemeat* of her enemies.

Lizzie stood up, feeling that by doing so she was at least showing willing.

It'd be all right if I knew what she *expected* me to do, she thought. After all, 'tis Saturday. Holidays, I thought Saturdays was meant to be.

'Is there any jobs you want doing?' she asked, because she really had no clues herself what she was supposed to be doing.

'Well, I daresay there would be,' said Patty, 'if I could think. And if you was to be *relied* on, Lizzie. Look at that half-pound of butter you left lying in the graveyard on'y last week. I *ask* you—butter in the graveyard! I should think it's on'y time there's been butter in graveyard since world began.'

'I ran straight back up for it,' protested Lizzie. 'Didn't come to no harm.'

'That ain't the point, Lizzie. It's the very *idea* of it. It nearly made me that I couldn't *fancy* it, knowing where it'd been.'

'Well is there anything *else?*' asked Lizzie desperately. '*Besides* errands.'

'Oh, do give over *pestering* me, Lizzie!' cried Patty, rummaging in the cupboard.

First I annoy her doing nowt, thought Lizzie. Now she don't want me to do owt. Can't do anything right.

She took advantage of Patty's turned back to slip out of the back door. She stood casting about for inspiration. Her eye fell on the riot of flowers round the little yard—dahlias and michaelmas daisies and a few roses.

That's what, she thought. I'll pick her a bunch of flowers and arrange 'em in that jug of hers shaped like a cat, and put 'em in front room. She'll like that.

She knew it was unlikely that Patty, engrossed in her baking, would look out through the tiny scullery window. All the same, she picked the flowers hastily, a few here, a few there, until she had a fair-sized bunch.

Now wait for her to go into't larder, or upstairs, she thought.

She peered cautiously through the crack in the open door. The kitchen was empty.

Upstairs! she thought jubilantly. She ran through the kitchen into the best room, and took the white cat jug (with tail curled up for handle) from its place on the mantelshelf. Hastily she ran back and filled it at the sink and put it on the draining board while she stuck the flowers in, curling rakishly over the cat's face.

She was halfway through when she heard Patty on the stairs. She grabbed the rest of the flowers, picked up the jug, and made across the kitchen. Her foot caught—in a crack in the lino—against the chair leg—she never knew which, and she pitched forward. The jug flew from her hand and fell with a smash smack at the feet of Patty herself, just come in.

Lizzie raised her head. Around her lay the strewn flowers, broken white pot, water. Above her was Patty's face, furious and disbelieving.

'That's my jug!' she cried. 'My best jug!'

'I was—I was putting flowers in it, for a surprise!' cried Lizzie, nearly sobbing now. 'And if you hadn't come down so quick I wouldn't have tripped and now—oh, I'm sorry, Mum, I'm sorry!'

Without answering, Patty went to the broom cupboard.

'Stand out way, Lizzie,' she said. 'Next thing, you'll have glass run in your feet.'

Lizzie watched her mother sweep the fragments into a dustpan, then she herself went and picked up the strewn flowers while Patty fetched the floor cloth and mopped up the water.

'That's that, then,' she said. 'And now what?'

'I've said I'm sorry, Mum,' said Lizzie. 'I *am* sorry. I tripped.'

'And you had to pick my best jug to do it with,' said Patty. 'That's what beats me. Couldn't have broke a jam jar, or that old brown pot of your grandmother's. You drive me to absolute *distraction*, Lizzie, I swear you do. You can't be turned back on five minutes together. That *baby's* more to be trusted to be left than you.'

She wouldn't carry on at me like this if she knew I'd got a *witch* for friend, Lizzie thought. She'd look out what she said to me, if she knew that.

For a moment, she was tempted to tell.

Fat lot of good that would do, she thought. Don't suppose she even believes in witches!

But remembering about the witch made her feel better, and gave her an idea.

I know what, she thought. I'll go and see if she's there. And if she is, I might get her to do a spell. What if she could do a spell so's Mum'd never find fault with me again, *ever*?

The idea was irresistible, beautiful. She got up.

'Just going out for a bit,' she said, and went out. Toby's pram was standing just under the window and she gave it a shove as she went by, and was rewarded by hearing his yells following her as she turned into the street.

'*Now* who's a little pettie pie?' she muttered under her breath. '*Now* who's Mummy's little fat lamb?'

As she passed through the rusted iron gate into the churchyard she willed the witch to be there.

Not all of them, she thought. Just mine.

She turned by the corner of the church, scanning cautiously about. It seemed important that she should see the witch before the witch saw her. At the moment, however, it did not seem as if either one thing or the other was likely to happen. She listened, and heard only the wind in the trees and dry grasses, and the far-off drone of a tractor.

'Witch!' she said softly. Then, a little louder, 'Witch! Witch, where are you?'

No reply. Lizzie's eyes raked the churchyard looking for a wisp of black, the tip of a pointed hat behind a tombstone, that might betray the witch's presence.

Could be playing hide and seek, she thought. She had seemed that kind of a witch.

'I see you!' came a shrill voice.

Lizzie jumped.

'I see you!' came the voice again.

'Well, I don't see you,' said Lizzie.

There was a cackle.

'Couldn't if you tried!' came the witch's triumphant voice. 'Invisible!'

'Couldn't you be visible, please?' said Lizzie. 'Just for a minute?'

No reply.

'Please?' said Lizzie.

Then she screamed. The witch *was* visible, and only a yard away, right under her nose and perched on the stone of *Betsy Mabel Glossop aged 79 years Life's Work Well Done.*

'That made you jump,' said the witch with satisfaction. Then, 'What do you want now?'

'Well—er . . . ' Lizzie was taken aback. She hardly liked to say it straight out, just like that.

'Well—er—for one thing, I wondered what your name was,' she said—perfectly truthfully, as it happened.

'Name?' snapped the witch. 'Not telling.'

'Oh!' said Lizzie.

'Don't want folk yelling my name all over from morning till night,' said the witch. She was beginning to sound like Patty herself. 'Might be invisible, but I ain't *deaf*, and if there's one thing I detest it's having folk yelling my name all over.'

'I'm sorry,' said Lizzie. 'All right, witch, don't tell me, if you don't want. But I did just wonder—well, I wondered if you'd do a little spell for me. Just a little one.'

'There ain't such things as little spells,' said the witch. 'Spells is big. *A l l* spells is big.'

'Well, then, a big one please, witch,' said poor Lizzie, beginning to feel more and more out of her depth. 'But it ain't a bad spell, witch. Not a wicked one—that's what I meant.'

'What, then?' demanded the witch.

'It's to do with my mum, see,' said Lizzie. 'Gone off me lately, she has. Telling me off the whole time—you know . . . '

69

'Why?' the witch enquired.

Lizzie shrugged.

'Dunno. Not my fault. Mostly because I left that dratted baby up at mill. *Anyone* could've made a mistake like that. Lucky thing is, Aunt Blodwen didn't see you, or there would've been trouble.'

'What spell d'ye want, then?' asked the witch. 'Turn baby into a toad, shall I?'

'Oh no!' Lizzie squealed with alarm. 'Don't do that! Please!'

She pictured Patty bending over the pram and seeing the transformed Toby under the string of plastic animals, and shuddered.

'Mum, then?' suggested the witch. 'Turn her toad, shall I?'

'No!' Lizzie fairly screamed. 'You've got it all wrong! I don't want *anyone* turning into toads! All I want is for you to make Mum like me a bit more, and—'

She broke off. The witch had vanished. Gone into thin air. Taken dudgeon.

'Witch? Are you still there?'

Silence.

'I bet you are!' cried Lizzie. 'So listen, please do! I just wanted you to put a spell on Mum so's to make her—well—you know—*like* me a bit more. Take more *notice*, instead of being always on about Toby. Witch? Witch . . . ?'

Silence. Then a swift glimpse of black rags, a blink of an eye in which she saw again the sharp face of the witch, and a snapped command, 'Do it yourself!' Then nothing.

Lizzie was too astonished to reply, even if there had been time.

'Witch!' she cried. 'Witch!'

This time, not only was there no reply, but Lizzie Dripping knew, deep in her heart, that there would be none.

Not even if I was to wait all day, she thought. All day and all night.

Slowly she turned away and began to walk back towards the gate. Even the witch had turned against her. She blinked hard.

Nobody cares, she thought. Nobody in the whole world.

She heard the witch's voice again: 'Do it yourself!'

She whipped round. No one was in sight. Then suddenly she found herself thinking. All right! I *will* do it myself!

And the way to do it was so perfectly simple that she laughed out loud and took several skipping steps down the path and back on to Kirk Street.

I'll get lost, she thought. I'll run away. And then they'll realize how much they love me, and be sorry. And they'll make a fuss over me like they did over Toby, and Mum'll never tell me off again for the rest of my life, not for *anything*.

And so Lizzie Dripping began to lay her plans. What she really planned was not to run away to the other side of the world for ever and ever, but just far enough and for long enough to make people—and Patty in particular—realize just how much they loved and missed her.

She saw no reason why she should starve while she was waiting to be found, so she took ten pence from her money box, gritted her teeth and marched up to the village shop. There she bought a chocolate biscuit, a bag of crisps, and a stock of bubble-gum. Back home, she mixed some orange squash and put it in a bottle. Up in her room she put everything into a carrier bag, along with a book to pass the time, and a torch in case it grew dark before she was found. Then she wrote her farewell note.

Mum'll be taking Toby for a push round the village in a bit, she thought. That's when I'll go. Nip out before Dad gets back from Mapleburn. Now, where's that letter?

She read it softly out, imagining the reactions of Patty and Albert when they found it lying there, and herself gone.

'*Dear Mum and Dad. I have run away from home,*

and shall not come back not for evermore. I know I am a big trouble to you and that is why I am going. You will still have Toby so you will be all right and not left orphaned. I will often think of you and goodbye for ever. Lizzie.'

It affected her so much that she had to brush away a tear from her own eye.

Then Patty called up: 'Going now, Lizzie!' and 'All right!' she called back, and then the house was quiet. Lizzie ran through into the front bedroom and watched Patty's back view disappearing. Then she took the bag and went downstairs.

And she went down as if it really were for the last time, stepping quite deliberately and aware of each familiar step, in the watery green and swaying light from the little window above the front door with its view of moving boughs.

She went tiptoe into the kitchen though there was no one there to see (unless the heavily ticking grandfather clock knew, minute by minute, the comings and goings of the Arbuckles, whose time it counted for them). She propped the note on the table, against the butter dish, unhooked her anorak from the back of the door, and went out.

Lizzie knew exactly where she was going. Just outside the village was a derelict barn. It was supposed to be haunted, but Lizzie, having met a witch, felt perfectly equal to a ghost. She marched steadily on and met only ancient Mrs Cobb, to whom she nodded and said, 'Hello.' As she reached the outskirts of Little Hemlock she could see the men at work in the ten-acre field beyond the beeches, but was certain that they could not see her.

She went through the mossed and broken five-barred gate into the weed-covered yard, took a last quick scan about to make sure no one was watching, and ran for the barn itself.

She crossed the threshold and there was sudden cool and shadowiness. There were quick stirs and patterings and she thought, Mice rats bats ghosts—help!

The barn seemed bigger and darker and quieter than any barn she had ever known before, and she wondered whether she had picked the right place for a hideout. Somewhere smaller would have felt safer, more homelike. But it was too late now.

She sat down and leaned against the doorpost. She took out the bottle and had a swig of the orange and felt a little better. Then she stared out at the empty yard and already felt as if she were the only person left alive in the world. Worse— she began to feel a little silly. So she opened a packet of gum and worked it up to a fine soft ball and began to blow bubbles, slowly and expertly, to keep herself company.

She looked at her watch and saw that it was only half-past four and wondered however she would pass the next couple of hours till it began to grow dark. She took out her book and immediately wished she had brought a different one. Giants seemed all too possible in that high, vacant barn. All the time she was reading she was aware of exactly where she was and what she was doing. She heard every single sound—the bleating of sheep, the muffled roar of cars passing, the odd scratchings and rustlings in the shadows behind her. She reached the end of chapter two, realized that she had not the least idea what the story was about and closed the book. Then she ate the crisps. Then the chocolate biscuit.

Wonder if they found the note yet? she thought.

And in the instant, a picture of the scene at home began to take shape in her mind . . .

Albert came in and hung his cap on the door as usual.

'Where's our Lizzie, then?' he asked.

'Lizzie? Come to think, don't know, Albert,' Patty replied frowning a little. 'Ain't seen her since dinner, come to think. Hiding out of my way, likely. Broke my best cat jug this morning, if you please.'

'Eeh, that's a right shame, Patty,' said Albert.

'Have to see if I can't get you another. Though jugs made like cats don't grow on trees, that's a fact. Liked that jug myself, I did—way his tail curled up to make handle. But the lass wouldn't do it o' purpose, not our Lizzie. Ain't seen her since dinner?'

'No.' Patty was a little alarmed now. 'No, I ain't.'

'Funny,' said Albert. 'Her off all this time and saying nowt.'

'I reckon I was too hard on the lass, looking back on it,' said Patty. 'She's a good lass, our Lizzie, when all's said and done. You don't—you don't reckon she's gone and done summat—summat silly, Albert?'

'What?' Now it was Albert's turn to be alarmed. 'Run off, you mean, or—wuss?'

'Oh!' cried Patty, wringing her hands. The baby outside began to yell but she hardly seemed to hear him. 'Oh, Albert, don't say such things. If owt should happen to our little lass, it'd break my heart. Fair break my heart!'

She lifted her head, saw the note, and in the instant snatched it up. Next minute she gave a despairing cry.

'Oh, Albert, Albert! I can't bear it! I can't!'

'What?' cried Albert. 'What is it?'

'She's gone!' Patty was sobbing now. 'Gone forever! Run off! It's all here, Albert! Oh, what've I done, what've I done?'

Silently Albert took the note and read it while his usually imperturbable face grew grim.

'I shall have to go after her,' he said. 'We'll ring police—get out search parties. We got to find that lass, Patty, we got to!'

'Oh, Albert!'—Patty was weeping unrestrainedly now— 'Don't leave me, don't! The dearest, sweetest child that ever a mother had, and I've drove her away! 'Twas me that drove her to it!'

Albert put an arm about her shoulders.

'There, lass, there. We'll find her.'

'If on'y she'll come back, if on'y we find her, I'll never say another wrong word to her again!' cried Patty, raising her tear-stained face. 'Never, as long as I live! Oh, Lizzie, Lizzie!'

* * *

77

The scene faded. Lizzie brushed a tear from her own eyes and a great hot wave of shame rushed over her from head to foot.

'Oh, Lizzie!' she whispered aloud. 'Oh, Lizzie Dripping, you *shouldn't* have!'

She had made a mistake. She knew it. In the very moment of knowing it, she got to her feet. And then she was running, running as fast as her legs would carry her, back towards home. And she was not running because she was lonely or scared or afraid of the approaching dusk (though she was all of these things), but because the thought of the hurt she had done to Patty and Albert was too much for her. And because she knew, quite certainly, that they did love her, and all the scoldings in the world would never change that.

She turned into Main Street and slowed down, out of breath.

Oh, Lizzie, what a fool you'll look! she thought, but she no longer cared.

She turned in at the gate and saw her father's van there and Toby's pram and everything just as it always was and yet somehow entirely different, as if she had been away for a thousand years. She went in through the open back door, saw Albert and Patty turn towards her, and she burst into tears.

'Here, then, here,' she heard her father say, and felt his arm about her shoulders. 'What's all this about?'

'Come along, petty,' she heard her mother say. 'You come and tell Mum what's the matter, then.'

Lizzie raised her wet face. 'Oh, Mum!' she cried. 'Dad! I'm sorry! I'm sorry!'

They stared.

'What is it?' asked Patty, and her voice was unusually gentle. 'What is it, then?'

It was then that Lizzie, looking beyond them, saw the note. There it stood, exactly where she had left it, propped against the butter dish. She leapt forward, snatched it up, and screwed it in her hand.

They need never know! she thought. They'll never know!

And what with the relief and one thing and another she began to laugh, so that she was laughing and crying at the same time, and she heard herself say: 'It don't matter, really it don't! There's nothing wrong, Mum, not now, really there ain't. And oh, Mum and Dad, I *do* love you!'

They still stood and still stared and in the silence Toby began to yell from his pram outside. Patty shook her head.

'Oh, Lizzie,' she sighed, 'Lizzie Dripping. Shall I ever understand you?'

And then Albert dug in his pocket and took out a little package and said, 'See what I brought you back from Mapleburn, Lizzie,' and Patty went out to fetch the baby, and the world was the right way up again.

Lizzie Dripping and the
Leek Nobblers

Albert Arbuckle, no mistake about it, was a leek man. For three years now he'd been Secretary of the Bilbury and Little Hemlock Leek Club. And he'd won second prize three times, third prize four times, and fourth prize twice. What he had never won, and what he dreamed of winning as most men dream of winning the pools, was First Prize. To be Actual Champion Leek Grower, to make leek history.

This particular year, he was certain in his very bones that in the little garden behind the cottage were growing leeks such as he had never grown before, leeks beautifully green above and thick and white and straight below—leeks to end all leeks.

It had all started as long ago as Boxing Day. It had been a good Christmas—a white one, if you count hoar frost as white—and Albert, who was a plumber, was looking forward to a New Year full of burst pipes.

'Freezing hard tonight,' he told Patty and Lizzie with satisfaction. He had just fetched in an armful of logs from the shed, and dumped them in the big basket by the hearth. He threw a couple on the fire and sat down, folding his arms, to watch them kindle and the sparks fly.

'Newspapers said mild,' remarked Patty, peeling an orange. 'Saw it in the papers. "Mild January expected," it said.'

'Never mind newspapers,' said Albert. 'They know nowt about it. There was Joe Banks in't Neville Arms last night. It'll freeze fleece off o't' sheep's backs, he says.'

'And he knows, Mum!' cried Lizzie. 'Joe Banks said it'd be fine for't anniversary outing, *and* it was! And he showed me some of his weather telling things—got 'em in his shed. He's got cones and feathers and all sorts. And a great big map wi' all the stars on it. 'Tain't a map of the world, it's a map o't *sky*.'

'*That's* more like sense,' said Albert. 'Them newspaper men in London, they're guessing at it, that's all. Got to take weather serious, like Joe does. You mark my words, Patty, there'll be more burst pipes this New Year than them newspapermen've had hot dinners.'

'Well,' said Patty, 'it's to be hoped you're right.'

'And if it *do* freeze on, there'll be skating!' cried Lizzie.

A knock came at the door. It was not so much a knock as a hammering, and a voice came above it.

'Albert! Are you there? Albert?'

Albert, a slow-moving man as a rule, leapt up and flung open the door.

'Oh! You is it,' said Patty. 'Come in, Jack, and get door shut.'

'Eeeh, Albert,' said Jack. 'Evening, Patty. Eeeeh, Albert, I don't like asking, not of a Boxing Day, but Albert, lad, I'm in a fair flummox at home.'

'Now steady up, Jack,' said Albert. 'You tell us, and we'll see what's to do.'

It turned out that a radiator was leaking in the Jacksons' bedroom. It had leaked right through the lino and floorboards and was now dripping on to the new carpet in the living-room. A regular brute of a leak, Jack said, just the kind of leak that *would* wait its time till Christmas to spring itself. Mrs Jackson was running back and forth with saucepans and buckets, crying her eyes out, and without a plumber, the pair of them would be up all night.

'If we was to go to bed and leave it,' said Jack, 'we should have house awash by morning. Furniture floating out through back door, I shouldn't wonder.'

'You get on back,' said Albert. 'I'm coming.'

'Pity, on Boxing Night,' remarked Patty, as Albert changed his slippers for his boots. 'There's the circus on't telly, and all.'

'Burst radiators is Acts of God, more nor less,' he said. 'Neither fire nor flood takes account of Boxing Day nor circuses nor owt else, that I know of. And Jack Jackson was champion leek grower this year—best for eleven year, they reckoned.'

'Oh, *that*!' said Patty, and Albert went out.

'Soft as grease, your father,' remarked Patty. 'Going out of a Boxing Night for that Jackson, as never has two pence to rub together, and'll not even offer to pay, if I know owt. And as for prize leeks, there's more to *that* than meets the eye.'

'What d'ye mean, Mum?'

'Nobbling,' said Patty grimly. 'There was

84

nobbling went on last year. Leeks got at in middle of night and spoilt, leeks dug up and vanished. I'd no more trust that Jack Jackson than I'd trust a barn rat.'

'Mum,' said Lizzie, 'if Jack Jackson had called their lad Jack, instead of Steve, would he've been Jack Jackson Jackson? And if he'd grown up and got married and had a boy, would he've been Jack Jackson Jackson Jackson?'

'Oh, for goodness' sake!' cried Patty. 'You could trust you to think of that, Lizzie Dripping!'

Makes sense, anyhow, thought Lizzie rebelliously. And she tried it out again in her mind. Jack Jackson Jackson Jackson . . .

When Albert came back, just over an hour later, Lizzie and Patty were sitting wide-eyed watching the television and absently munching peanuts. Neither of them so much as turned round. He took off his coat and cap and hung them behind the door.

'All right now, is it?' asked Patty, without taking her eyes off the screen. 'I swear that acrobat'll break his neck, he—ooooh!'

She and Lizzie screamed together.

'Ooooh! I can hardly bring myself to look!' cried Patty, craning forward.

'Oh, Patty,' said Albert, standing there. 'Oh, lass!'

Lizzie, struck by something in his voice, did turn, and saw a look on her father's face that she had never seen there before.

'What? What is it, Dad?'

Slowly Albert came forward. He seemed dazed, as if he had seen a vision. And he had. He had seen a vision of leeks of such whiteness, of such length and thickness, of such sheer beauty, that they might have been grown in Paradise itself.

'Oh, lass!' he said again. 'See here!'

With his thumb and finger he dug into his waistcoat pocket and fetched out a small paper packet. Shaking his head, he sat heavily in his chair, and carefully shook the contents of the packet into the palm of his hand.

The others stared.

'Pips!' Lizzie cried. 'Leek pips!'

Albert himself sat staring at them as if they might sprout to life then and there in the palm of his hand, as if one miracle had already happened and another was about to at any minute.

'They're Jack's,' he said, still staring down. 'Them leeks of his last year—six inches round and eleven and three-eighths long! *Them* leeks!'

He looked back at Patty and Lizzie now.

'Didn't have no cash, see,' he explained. 'Couldn't pay owt. Spent up for Christmas.'

'And that's just like him,' put in Patty. 'Could've told you that, Albert.'

'I stopped his leak,' said Albert, 'and he give me these.'

'A leek for a leak!' cried Lizzie. 'Get it? Fair exchange is no robbery. A leek for a leak!'

And that was how it all began, with a palmful of pips from Jack Jackson's champion leeks. 'Worth their weight in gold,' so Albert declared, and guarded them accordingly. And when the time came, he planted them in his tiny greenhouse with exquisite care, each inside an empty toilet roll.

'To make 'em come straight, ain't it, Dad?' enquired Lizzie, who had come to watch the ceremony of the planting. She herself had come to believe that there was something extraordinary, even magical, about these particular pips, even though to her they looked exactly like any of the others she had ever seen.

Albert nodded. He was too intent on his task to speak—pressing the earth firmly yet reverently with his thumbs. He took another trowelful of earth from the large box by his feet.

'And that's special soil, ain't it, Dad?' said Lizzie. 'Is it same recipe as last year?'

Again Albert nodded. 'Near enough. Though I tell you what, lass. I'm giving it a try, this year.'

'Giving what a try, Dad?'

Albert looked left and right, as if expecting to see an eavesdropper lurking, and lowered his voice.

'Epsom salts!'

'Epsom salts?' cried Lizzie loudly, then clapped a hand to her mouth as Albert again looked nervously about him.

'Aye. It'll fair make 'em dance, will that. It's Bill Mason always swears by it—and he comes into top ten year after year. Give 'em Epsom salts, he says, and you can wash your hands on 'em for't rest of year. Fair makes 'em dance, he says.'

He's gone daft in the head! thought Lizzie. Epsom salts? Make 'em *dance*? Poor old Dad. And what if he don't win?

A terrible thought struck her, remembering Patty's dark hints about Jack Jackson and last year's nobbled leeks.

'They are *really* champion pips, ain't they, Dad?' she said. 'I mean, he wouldn't *cheat* on you?'

Albert chuckled.

'They're champion, all reet,' he said. ' 'Twas his missus thought on it, see. "You ain't got no money, you give Albert some o' those pips o' yourn you're saving," she says. And out she nips and fetches 'em before Jack so much as had time to blink. Mind, you should've seen his face— dropped a mile. Would've stood with his finger stopping that leak all night rather'n part with them pips, you could see that!'

'So you really could beat 'em all this year, then, Dad,' Lizzie said. 'First prize, Albert Arbuckle. Champion Leek Grower. Champion Leek Grower in the World!'

'Well now, Lizzie,' said Albert, 'between us two, I might at that—Bilbury and Little Hemlock Champion, any road. But best keep mum, see.'

'Why?'

Again Albert looked around him.

'Nobblers.' His voice was low. 'You'd not believe what some'll get up to, Lizzie. Poisoning and stealing and—'

Patty came in through the greenhouse door and they both jumped.

'Oh, Mum!' cried Lizzie.

'Look as if you'd seen a ghost, pair of you,' Patty said.

'Dad was telling about nobbling!' cried Lizzie. 'Folks creeping up and murdering leeks at dead of night. Kidnapping 'em, too. *Leek* napping. What's that letter, Mum?'

'From my old Aunt Bertha,' said Patty. 'At Winkbeck.'

'What about her?' demanded Lizzie.

'Rheumatics, mostly,' Patty said. 'Can't hardly stir, she says, poor old woman. Shall you keep an eye on things here, Albert, if I get over and see her? I should take Toby.'

'Eh, well, if that's what you want, Patty.'

'Getting morbid in the head, by sounds of it,' said Patty. 'Going on about being buried next Uncle Arthur. And the way them two went on hammer and tongs at each other forty year! I shall catch half-past-ten bus, and be back five-ish. There's pie in't pantry and tomatoes, and you'll see what else if you have a rummage.'

'Right, then,' said Albert. 'Though I could drive you over in the van, if you'd a mind.'

She turned again at the door.

'And when I do get back,' she said, 'I dare say I shall be ready for a cup of tea.'

'Aye, Patty. We shall see to't, shan't we, Lizzie?'

Then she was gone. The pair of them looked at one another like conspirators.

'What shall we do, Dad?' asked Lizzie. 'When you've done putting pips in, I mean?'

'You wait on a bit,' Albert told her. 'Don't rush me. I'll think o' summat.'

And he did. Once the pips were sown and the greenhouse door locked behind them, they set off in the van for Kipton Market. They had their dinner at a hot dog stall, bought five different kinds of fertilizer, and set off back in plenty of time to get tea ready. By five o'clock they were sitting there, the table laid with bread and butter and the cream cakes they'd bought, and the kettle singing.

'That'll be her now,' said Albert, and at almost the same moment they heard Patty's voice.

'Albert! Albert?'

He and Lizzie made for the door and Lizzie threw it open. There stood Patty, red and flustered, Toby tucked under one arm and with the other hand clutching a lead on the other end of which was a large, shaggy, panting sheepdog.

'Towser!' yelled Lizzie. 'It's old Towser!'

'Here,' said Albert, 'let's have him,' and he took Toby. Lizzie snatched at the lead.

'What's he come for, Mum?' she cried. 'Are we to have him? Is Auntie Bertha dead?'

'Might as well be,' said Patty gloomily, 'for all she's able to do for herself. And *half* dead's what *I* am, near enough, managing them two on the bus. The one yowling and t'other tugging fit to pull my arm off.'

'Bad is she, then?' asked Albert.

'Got to go in a Home,' said Patty. 'And no dogs allowed. You don't think I'd've brought

that great prancing nuisance back here else, do you?'

'To stop?' shrieked Lizzie. 'Is he to stop?'

'As if we'd room for *him*,' Patty went on. 'Eat us out of house and home, I shouldn't wonder. But a promise is a promise, and that's all there is to it.'

'Oh!' breathed Lizzie. 'He *is* to stay!'

'Might even do a bit o' good,' murmured Albert. 'Watchdog, like.'

'For the leeks!' cried Lizzie. '*You* won't let 'em come creeping round nobbling Dad's leeks, will you, Towser? Ooooh, you're a grand, smashing old dog,' and she rubbed her face against his and felt his tail wagging against her.

Then Patty said, 'What about that cup of tea, then?' and they all went in and the whole thing was settled.

For the next month or two Lizzie was so taken up with her own affairs, and especially with Towser, that she gave Albert's leeks hardly a thought. Then May came, and with it the time for planting the young leeks out of doors. This, Lizzie knew, was the most important part of all. The weather had to be right, and so did the soil in the trenches. Lizzie watched Albert stirring his ingredients together in a wooden barrel—a spadeful of this, a trowel of that, the merest pinch of the other—for all the world like a wizard bent over a magic brew. Except that wizards as a rule do not wear cloth caps.

'And now there's just one thing, Lizzie,' he told her, straightening slowly. 'Sheep droppings.'

Lizzie knew all about this. Whatever else went into the mixture each year, from sawdust to eiderdowns and Epsom salts, the sheep droppings were a must.

'I'll take Towser and go along with you,' she said. Albert fetched his wheelbarrow and the pair of them set off down Main Street towards the ten-acre where Farmer Stokes kept his sheep.

They rounded a sharp bend in the lane and met Jack Jackson head on—in fact *bang* on—one wheelbarrow right into the other. Jack's wheelbarrow was full of sheep droppings.

'Morning, Jack,' said Albert.

'Morning, Albert.'

'Fine day.'

'It is that.'

'Got your droppings, then?'

'Aye. You off up there now, are you?'

'Aye.'

There was a pause.

'Leeks coming along all right then, are they?' enquired Jack carelessly.

'Fairish,' said Albert, deadpan. 'Fair to middling.'

That's right, Dad, thought Lizzie. Don't you tell him!

'Rum do, you and me growing from same pips,' said Jack.

'Pips is same,' agreed Albert. 'All in the growing of 'em now, you might say. Best man to win.'

If there ain't any nobbling, thought Lizzie.

'Got a dog, Albert, I see,' said Jack. He bent to pat Towser. 'Don't bite, do he?'

'Not as I know of,' said Albert, and 'He might!' said Lizzie, both at the same time.

'Good boy,' said Jack, drawing back his hand.

Don't you go making friends with him,

Towser, thought Lizzie fiercely. You get ready to *bite* him, if needs be!

'Morning, then,' said Jack Jackson, picking up the handles of the barrow.

'Morning, Jack.'

And Lizzie and Albert went on their way to spend the morning shovelling up sheep droppings and hearing the cuckoos call about them.

The days went by, the weeks and months, and Albert's leeks grew tall and green and beautiful— though the size of the *real* part, the part that was underground, they could only guess at. And every night Towser slept in the shed, with the door open, so that he could rush out and bite nobblers, if needs be.

But then came August, and the Arbuckles were to go and stay in a caravan by the sea for a week, and Towser with them. As the day for their departure grew nearer, Albert grew glummer and glummer. You would have thought he had booked in for his own funeral, instead of a holiday.

'As sure as we sit here, Patty,' he said gloomily at supper, the evening before they were due to go, 'we shall get back here and find them leeks gone. And if we don't find 'em gone, we shall find 'em with leaves gone yellow, or tops cut off. *Summat* awful we shall find.'

'We can't stop our holiday for leeks, Albert,' said Patty. 'They've been all right other years, ain't they?'

'Didn't have champion pips other years, Patty,' Albert reminded her.

'Well, you never mind,' Patty told him. 'You set altogether too much store on them leeks, Albert. And if they don't win't prize, we can always eat 'em. Leek puddings in suet—makes your mouth water to think on it. Think o' that, Albert.'

Albert shuddered and said nothing.

Poor Dad, thought Lizzie. He'd choke, eating leek dumplings, if he don't win prize. But what's to do?

She had a thought.

What about witch? Hmmmm . . . Never helped before, mind you, but you never know. Might help if she'd a *mind* to. That's it. I'll ask her!

She slipped out into the warm, hay-smelling twilight and made for the churchyard, Towser at her heels. As she stepped through the little iron gate into the graveyard itself, the light seemed suddenly to dim, all in a moment, and the air to chill. Lizzie shivered, and said to herself, '*I* ain't frit, not me! Sun's dropped, that's all.'

But the graveyard in the twilight was not at all the same thing as it was in the day-time. And looking about her at the still grass and absolutely silent and fixed gravestones, Lizzie felt perfectly certain that her witch was nowhere about. She was not even *invisibly* not there. She realized something else, too.

My ole witch ain't got nothing to do with Dad's leeks, she thought. She's only really got to do with *me*. Don't mix, witches and leeks.

She took a last look and a last deep breath of the peacefulness, then went back, closed the gate behind her, and scrambled down the bank by the memorial cross. As she did so, a car went by. It had a roof rack stacked high with suitcases, deckchairs, and folding stools. In the half-light, Lizzie glimpsed pale faces.

'Jack Jackson!' she shrieked out loud. 'Oh, stone the crows—it's him!'

She raced full tilt back on home where Albert and Patty were pushing the last things into baskets and carrier bags.

'It's all right!' she shrieked. 'They've gone! They've gone on *their* holidays! I just seen 'em!'

'Who?' demanded Patty. 'And keep your voice down, do. Only just got *him* off. Seen who?'

'The Jacksons! Him and her and Steve in the

back and luggage on the roof as if they was going to't north pole! They're off, Dad! Gone!'

Slowly Albert rose to his feet.

'Well, bless my soul!' he said. 'If that don't beat all!'

Crikey! thought Lizzie. *Was* the witch there?

And it seemed for an instant, even in the familiar, lamplit kitchen, that she might have been, after all—might just, *just* have had a hand in it all.

'Well, that'll keep you from grizzling all week about your blessed leeks,' said Patty to Albert. '*I* could do with a holiday from 'em, if you can't.'

'We could even go up there now and nobble *his* leeks!' said Lizzie, wicked and reckless with relief.

'Now then, Lizzie,' said Albert. 'You know better than that.'

'And you get off upstairs, quick,' said Patty. 'Running off out at a time like this. Early start tomorrow, and well you know it.'

So Lizzie went to bed, and she dreamed that Jack Jackson came creeping up at dead of night to nobble Albert's leeks, and that Towser threw back his head and barked fit to wake the dead, and that the witch came suddenly out of nowhere, and whoosh! changed Jack Jackson into a toad there and then and for evermore!

Patty did not dream at all—she never did. But Albert, he dreamed of leeks that grew, and grew, and grew, and grew, till they were so enormous that there was no room in his head for anything else, and he woke up.

And in September, at the Bilbury and Little Hemlock Leek Show, the truth was better than anyone's dreams. Lizzie herself stood all morning by Albert's three leeks on the long trestle table, guarding them, and jealously comparing them with all the other entries as they were brought in. And she had already awarded Albert first prize in her own head before the judging had even started.

Then, at half past two, the announcement was made. A hush fell in the little hall as the judge, a sheet of paper in his hand, mounted the rostrum. At a Leek Show, Lizzie knew, *everyone* gets a prize. And this year there had been seventy-three entries. The judge started with seventy-third prize—a glass butter dish—and began to work his way down.

The Arbuckles had stood like this, waiting, many times before, but never before had the list seemed so long. Fiftieth came, twentieth, tenth— and now a stir ran through the crowd. Here, in the top ten, were the real honours—and the big prizes, the electric irons, the tea services, the lawn mowers.

'Third Prize,' said the judge, 'Jack Jackson. A portable radio.'

'Ooooh!' Lizzie let out a long-held breath. 'You've done it, Dad!' she whispered, and took a sideways look at Albert's deadpan face, only a red flush above his collar betraying his emotion.

'Second Prize, Percy Green. A portable record player, with record tokens to't value of ten pound.'

'Oooooh, *Albert*!' It was Patty herself now, leek fever running in her veins at last, converted.

'And First Prize,' the judge stared gravely at his list, spinning the moment out. 'First Prize, and title of Champion Leek Grower of the Bilbury and Little Hemlock Leek Club 1972—Albert Arbuckle!'

'Oh, Dad!' Lizzie felt gooseflesh break out all over, and Patty gave him a little push and the pair of them stood mazed to watch Albert, in his best suit and cap in hand, walk deliberately up on to the platform amid a roar of applause and a stamping of boots. The judge raised his hand, and silence fell.

'First Prize,' said the judge, 'The Silver Trophy' (he held it aloft) 'and an electric washing machine!'

'Ooooooh!' Patty's shriek was audible. Albert, finding all of a sudden that he needed one hand to shake the judge's and another to take the trophy, stuffed his cap hastily into his pocket.

Lizzie, watching, felt a lump rise in her throat.

Dreams *do* come true, she thought. Don't care if they *do* call me Lizzie Dripping. I believe in dreams, I do!

And then she clapped her hands with the rest until they stung, and shouted hurray, and didn't care a hoot who saw her, because she was clapping for Albert and clapping for Albert's dream and for *all* dreams. And most of all, for dreams that come true . . .